A HARRY
the Dirty Dog
TREASURY

Three stories by Gene Zion
pictures by Margaret Bloy Graham

CONTENTS

BARNES
&NOBLE
BOOKS
NEW YORK

HARRY

by Gene Zion

the Dirty Dog

Pictures by **Margaret Bloy Graham**

Harry was a white dog with black spots
who liked everything,
except ... getting a bath.
So one day when he heard the water
running in the tub,
he took the scrubbing brush ...

and buried it in the back yard.

Then he ran away from home.

He played where they were fixing the street

and got very dirty.

He played at the railroad

and got even dirtier.

He played tag with other dogs

and became dirtier still.

He slid down a coal chute
and got the dirtiest of all.
In fact, he changed

from a white dog with black spots,
to a black dog with white spots.

Although there were many other things to do, Harry began to wonder if his family thought that he had <u>really</u> run away.

He felt tired and hungry too,
so without stopping on the way
he ran back home.

When Harry got to his house,
he crawled through the fence
and sat looking at the back door.

One of the family looked out and said,
"There's a strange dog in the back yard...
by the way, has anyone seen Harry?"

When Harry heard this, he tried very hard
to show them <u>he</u> was Harry. He started to do
all his old, clever tricks. He flip-flopped

and he flop-flipped.
He rolled over and played dead.

He danced and he sang.

He did these tricks over and over again,
but everyone shook his head and said,
"Oh, no, it couldn't be Harry."

Harry gave up
and walked slowly toward the gate,
but suddenly he stopped.

He ran to a corner of the garden
and started to dig furiously.
Soon he jumped away from the hole
barking short, happy barks.

He'd found the scrubbing brush!
And carrying it in his mouth,
he ran into the house.

Up the stairs he dashed,
with the family
following close behind.

He jumped into the bathtub and sat up begging,
with the scrubbing brush in his mouth,
a trick he certainly had never done before.

"This little doggie wants a bath!"
cried the little girl, and her father said,
"Why don't you and your brother give him one?"

Harry's bath was the soapiest one he'd ever had.
It worked like magic. As soon as the children
started to scrub, they began shouting,
"Mummy! Daddy! Look, look! Come quick!"

"It's Harry! It's Harry! It's Harry!" they cried.
Harry wagged his tail and was very, very happy.
His family combed and brushed him lovingly, and
he became once again a white dog with black spots.

It was wonderful to be home.
After dinner, Harry fell asleep
in his favorite place, happily dreaming
of how much fun it had been getting dirty.
He slept so soundly,
he didn't even feel the scrubbing brush
he'd hidden under his pillow.

No Roses for
HARRY!

No Roses for

by Gene Zion

HARRY!

Pictures by Margaret Bloy Graham

NO ROSES FOR HARRY!
Text copyright © 1958 by Eugene Zion
Text copyright renewed 1986 by Ruth Zion Frischer
Illustrations copyright © 1958 by Margaret Bloy Graham
Illustrations copyright renewed 1986 by Margaret Bloy Graham
All rights reserved. No part of this book may be
used or reproduced in any manner whatsoever without
written permission except in the case of brief quotations
embodied in critical articles and reviews.
For information address
HarperCollins Children's Books, a division of HarperCollins
Publishers, 10 East 53rd Street, New York, NY 10022.

Library of Congress catalog card number: 58-7752
ISBN 0-06-026890-5
ISBN 0-06-026891-3 (lib. bdg.)
ISBN 0-06-443011-1 (pbk.)

Harry was a white dog with black spots.
On his birthday, he got a present from Grandma.
It was a woolen sweater with roses on it.
Harry didn't like it the moment he saw it.
He didn't like the roses.

When he tried it on, he felt cosy and snug.
But he still didn't like the roses.
He thought it was the silliest sweater
he'd ever seen.

The next day when Harry went downtown
with the children, he wore his new sweater.
When people saw it, they laughed.
When dogs saw it, they barked.
Harry made up his mind then and there
to lose Grandma's present.

When they went into a big store to shop,
the children took off his sweater and let him
carry it. This was just what Harry wanted.

First he tried to lose it in the pet department —

but a man found it and gave it back.

Then he tried to lose it in the grocery department—

but a lady found it and gave it back.

He tried to lose it in the flower department—

but a little boy found it and gave it back.

The children didn't let Harry carry it any more.
They made him wear it. As they started home,
Harry was beginning to think he'd never lose it.

When he got home, his friends were waiting
to play with him. But Harry didn't feel like
playing so they left him alone.

As he sat wondering what to do,
Harry noticed a loose stitch in his sweater.
He pulled at the wool—just a little at first—
then a bit more—and a little bit more.
Harry didn't know it, but a bird was watching.

In a minute, Harry had pulled out
quite a long piece of the wool.
The end of it lay on the grass behind him.
Suddenly the bird flew down.

Quick as a flash she took the end of the wool
in her beak and flew away with it!
It all happened before Harry could even blink.

The sweater began to disappear right before Harry's eyes. First one leg—then the neck—

then the other leg—then the back—and finally

the whole thing was just one long, long piece of
wool flying off into the sky. The sweater was gone!
Harry could hardly believe it.

He barked and jumped with joy!
Then he ran out of the yard.

He ran down the street barking thank you
to the bird over and over again.

The bird and wool were just a tiny speck in
the sky, but Harry kept following them.

He came home thirsty and tired, and was having
a drink in the kitchen when the children ran in.
"We got a letter from Grandma!" one of them said.
"She's coming to visit us!" shouted the other.
Harry thought of the sweater and his tail drooped.

Before Grandma came, the family looked everywhere
for the sweater. They wanted her to see how nice
Harry looked in it. Of course they couldn't find it.
Only Harry knew why.

When Grandma arrived, Harry ran to her with
his leash. Then he sat up and begged.
"All right, Harry," said Grandma. "After I've had
my lunch and a nap, we'll go for a walk."

That afternoon, Harry and Grandma and the children
started off on their walk. Harry barked happily
and pulled towards the park.

When they got to the park, Harry pulled harder. The children let him off his leash and he ran on ahead. He seemed to be looking for something.

All at once, he stopped under a big tree.
He looked up and began to bark and wag his tail.
Grandma and the children came running.

They got to the tree and looked up too.
Suddenly one of the children said, "I see a <u>nest</u>!"
"It's made of <u>wool</u>!" said the other,
"and it's the <u>very</u> <u>same</u> <u>color</u> as—"
"<u>Harry's</u> <u>sweater</u>!" they shouted together.

"It is Harry's sweater!" exclaimed Grandma.
Just then a bird looked out of the nest.
"Look! Grandma, look!" shouted the children.
"Harry gave his sweater to a bird!"
"I wonder how he did that!" said Grandma.
The bird sang and Harry wagged his tail even harder.

At Christmas, Harry got a present from Grandma.
It was a <u>new</u> sweater!
Harry liked this one very much.
When he tried it on, he felt as cosy and snug
as the bird in the nest.
But best of all—it was white with black spots!

HARRY
by the Sea

HARRY

by Gene Zion

by the Sea

Pictures by **Margaret Bloy Graham**

Harry was a white dog with black spots
who liked everything about the seashore,
except...the hot sun.
One day when the sun was hotter than ever,
Harry looked for a shady place to sit.
But when he tried to get under
the family's beach umbrella...

it was too crowded and the family made him leave.

When he crawled into the children's sand castle...

the walls fell in and the children chased him away.

When he walked in the shade that a fat lady made...

she became angry and made him stop following her.

"Get lost!" she said. She was very annoyed.

The sun was very hot and Harry had walked
a long way from the main beach.
He was tired, so he sat down at the water's edge.

All of a sudden a big wave came from behind
and crashed right on top of him.

When the wave rolled back, Harry was left floating
in the water. He was completely covered with seaweed.
He didn't look like a dog anymore—
he looked like something from the bottom of the sea.

Suddenly a lady saw him floating toward her.
"Help! Help!" she shrieked. "It's a Sea Monster!"
The lifeguard heard her and blew his whistle.
"Everybody out!" he shouted. "Everybody out!"

Everyone ran out of the water, and so did Harry.
He was still covered with cold, wet seaweed.
It made him feel cool and comfortable, and now
he didn't mind the sun at all. He felt so good,
he started running back to his family.

On his way, some people saw him.
"It's a Sea Serpent!" one of them screamed.
"It's a Giant Sandworm!" shrieked another.
Harry had water in his ears and could hardly hear them.
He kept on running toward the main beach.

When he got there, Harry stopped and stared. Instead of
just his family's umbrella, now there were hundreds
of them. They were <u>all</u> striped—just like his family's.
Harry couldn't tell one umbrella from another.

Suddenly two beach attendants saw him.
"Holy smoke!" one of them gasped. "What's that?"
"It's a Bushy-backed Sea Slug!" exclaimed the other.
They whispered for a moment. Then they ran.

Harry went from umbrella to umbrella, but he couldn't find his family. <u>Everyone</u> wore sun hats and sunglasses, and <u>everyone</u> used suntan oil—just like his family. Harry looked and sniffed very hard, but it was no use. He couldn't tell one family from another.

Suddenly the two beach attendants came running back
carrying a big trash basket. They ran toward Harry.
"Stand back!" one of them said to the crowd.
"We're going to catch it and take it to the Aquarium!"
said the other.

Then they tiptoed right up behind Harry
and raised the trash basket over his head.
Harry didn't know the beach attendants were
behind him. He was listening to something.

He thought he heard someone calling his name.
There it was again. "Harry! Harry! Harry!"
Now Harry was sure. He didn't wait another second.
Just as the basket came down—

he ran! He ran right out from under the basket!
It happened so fast, the beach attendants
just stood there with their mouths open.

As he raced through the crowd some people screamed, some people ran, and some people did both. But Harry paid no attention. He kept on running across the beach.

When he got to the Hot Dog stand,
he stopped and barked happily.
Behind the counter the Hot Dog man was shouting.
It was <u>his</u> voice that Harry had heard. But Harry had
water in his ears and couldn't hear very well.

The man wasn't shouting, "Harry! Harry! Harry!"
He was shouting, "Hurry! Hurry! Hurry! Get 'em while
they're hot!" Harry still thought the man was
calling his name. He barked and jumped with joy.
He jumped so much that suddenly...

the seaweed all fell off!
When the crowd saw that Harry was a dog,
they gasped. They could hardly believe their eyes.
All at once Harry began to jump higher than ever.

He saw the children! They were running toward him.
"Oh, Harry!" they cried. "We heard you bark!"
"We've been looking all over for you!"
Harry was so happy, he did a little dance.

The Hot Dog man was very grateful to Harry
for bringing the crowd to his stand. He sold all
the hot dogs he had. He gave Harry a free hamburger.
The lady who had told Harry to "get lost" came along
and bought him a cold drink.

"You're no Sea Monster," she said. "You're just a lost,
hot dog." Everyone laughed except the two children.
"He's <u>not</u> lost!" one of them said.
"He's <u>Harry</u> and he's <u>ours</u>!"
Then they hurried off to join the rest of the family.

The next time Harry's family went to the beach,
they brought a new umbrella. Harry liked this one
very much. It was white with black spots.
No matter how crowded the beach became,
it was easy to find. But best of all — it was big,
and when the sun got very hot,
there was room underneath for them all.